For Joanna, Elena, and Henry, the greatest gifts we ever received
—A.G. & A.S.G.

For Roslyn
—D.S.

Dial Books for Young Readers
An imprint of Penguin Random House LLC, New York

Visit us online at penguinrandomhouse.com

ISBN 9781984815460

Printed in China
10 9 8 7 6 5 4 3 2 1

Design by Mina Chung • Text set in Zemke Hand ITC
The art was created using ink and watercolor,
with digital modifications.

THE GIFT INSIDE THE BOX

Adam Grant and Allison Sweet Grant

and illustrator Diana Schoenbrun

 Dial Books for Young Readers

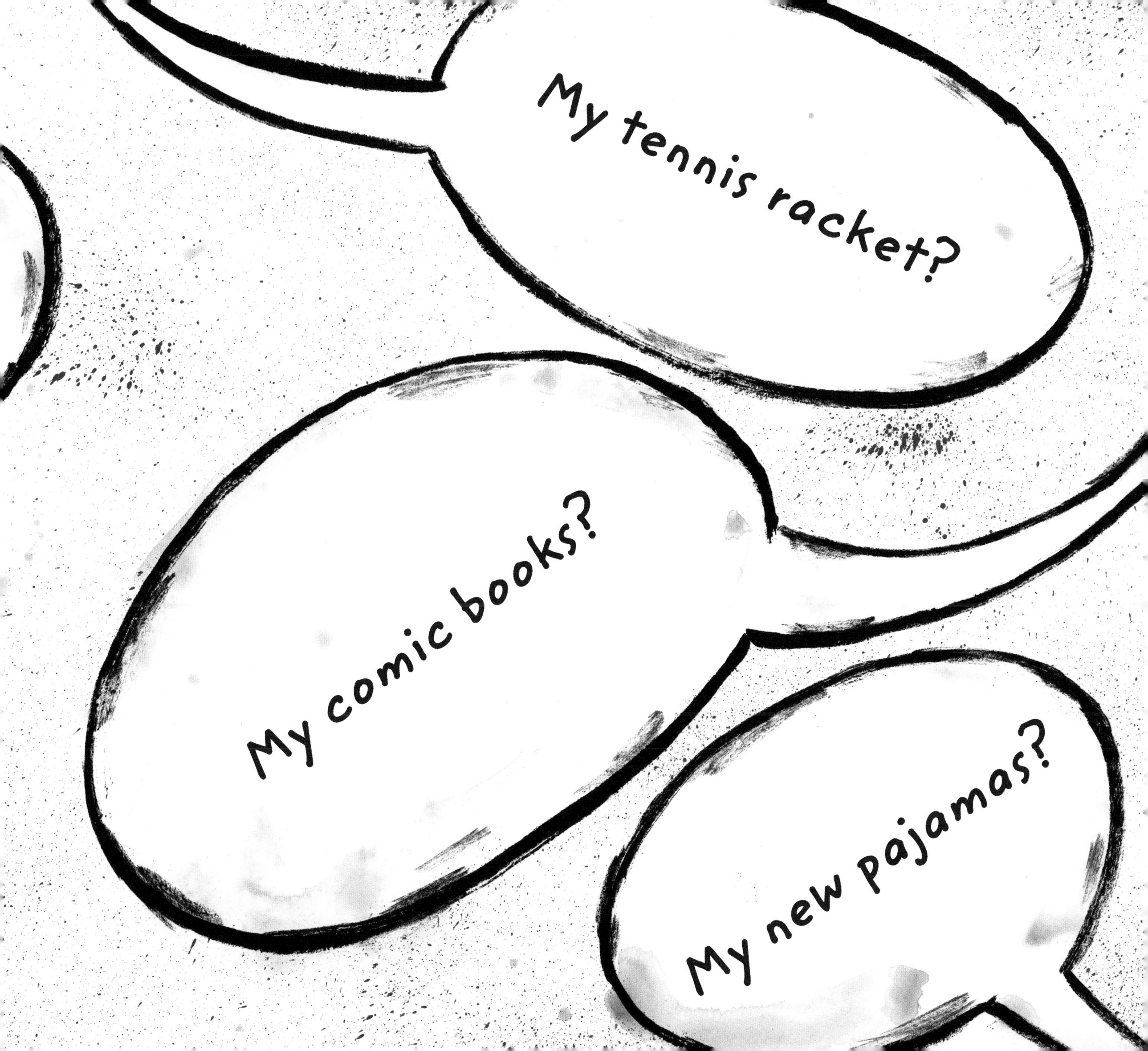
My tennis racket?
My comic books?
My new pajamas?

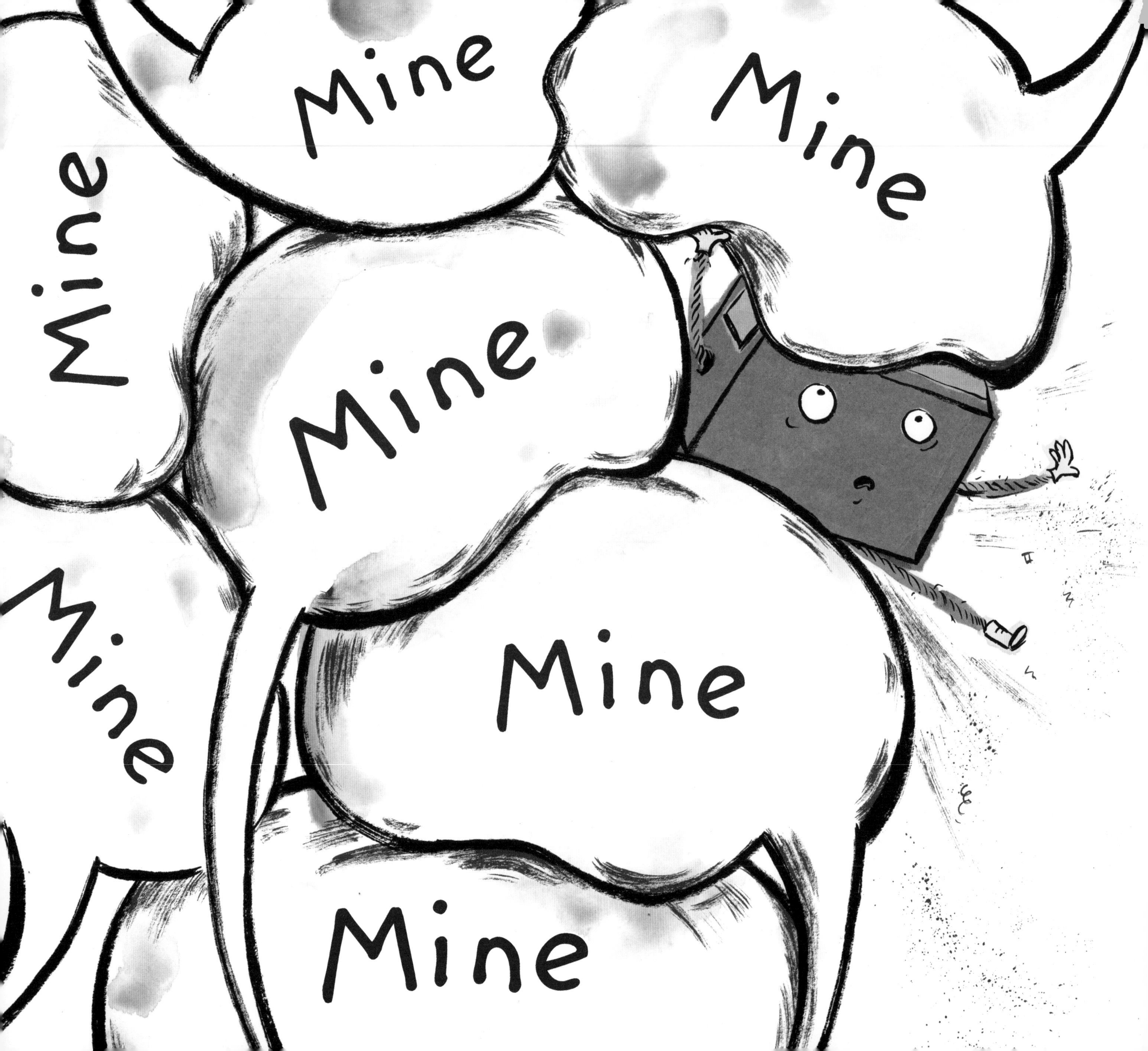
Mine
Mine
Mine
Mine
Mine
Mine
Mine

Who would YOU give this box to?